D0577565

Rebecca Bond

Charlesbridge

For Arnold Lobel,
and for the children of Saint Ann's School in Brooklyn,
both of whom inspired me to write an early reader

–R. B.

Published by Charlesbridge
85 Main Street
Watertown, MA 02472
(617) 926-0329
www.charlesbridge.com

Library of Congress Cataloging-in-Publication Data
Names: Bond, Rebecca, 1972–author.
Title: Pig and Goose and the first day of spring / Rebecca Bond.
Description: Watertown, MA: Charlesbridge, [2017] | Summary: On the first day of spring Pig sets out to have a picnic by the pond, meets Goose, and so discovers a new friend.
Identifiers: LCCN 2016013778 | ISBN 9781580895941 (reinforced for library use) | ISBN 9781607347156 (ebook) | ISBN 9781607348467 (ebook pdf)
Subjects: LCSH: Swine—Juvenile fiction. | Geese—Juvenile fiction. | Friendship—Juvenile fiction. | Picnics—Juvenile fiction. | Spring—Juvenile fiction. | CYAC: Pigs—Fiction. | Geese—Fiction. | Friendship—Fiction. | Picnics—Fiction. | Spring—Fiction.
Classification: LCC PZ7.B63686 Pi 2017 | DDC [E]—dc23
LC record available at https://lccn.loc.gov/2016013778

Printed in China
(hc) 10 9 8 7 6 5 4 3 2 1

Illustrations done in watercolor and ink on watercolor paper
Display type set in Aunt Mildred by Akemi Aoki/MvB Design
Text type set in Berkeley by International Typeface Corporation
Color separations by Colourscan Print Co Pte Ltd, Singapore
Printed by 1010 Printing International Limited in Huizhou, Guangdong, China
Production supervision by Brian G. Walker
Designed by Diane M. Earley

Contents

A Spring Morning

It was spring at last.
Pig was in a good mood.
"The sun is shining!" said Pig.
"The sky is blue!" said Pig.
"Goody gumdrops!" said Pig.
"I am going to have a picnic by the pond."

Pig packed a big lunch and set off.
She began to skip.
She began to hum.
Then she stopped.
Up above, in the clear blue sky,
there was a small white dot.

The dot got bigger

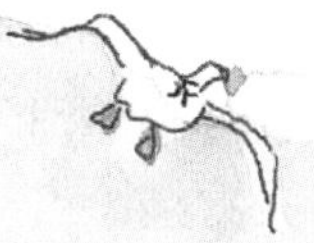

and bigger.

The dot came to land right by Pig!
The dot was not a dot at all.

It was a goose!

"Hello," said Pig. "I am Pig."

"Good morning," said Goose. "I am Goose."

"Wow, Goose," Pig said with a sigh.

"How *well* you fly!"

Goose blushed.

"Shucks," he said. "It is nothing."

"Oh yes!" cried Pig.

"It *is* something. I wish *I* could do that!"

"It is not hard," said Goose.

"Maybe I could teach you."

"Really?" said Pig. "*Me*?"

"Yes," said Goose, "why not?"

"Ooh!" squealed Pig. "Goody gumdrops!"

"To begin," said Goose,
"you need to run fast, like this."
Goose started to run.
"To begin," said Pig,
"I need to run fast, like this."
Pig started to run, too.

“Next!” shouted Goose,
“flap your arms, like this!”
Goose flapped his wings.

“Next!” shouted Pig,
“flap my arms, like this!”
Pig flapped her arms.

"Last," yelled Goose,
"let the wind lift you up, like this!"
"Last," yelled Pig,
"let the wind lift me up, like this!"

Pig waited for the wind to lift her up.

The wind did not lift her up.
"I will run faster!" thought Pig.
"I will flap harder!" thought Pig.

Still, the wind did not lift her up.

Soon Pig was panting.
She had to slow down.
She had to stop.
Pig bent over and took many gulps of air.
"Ahhh!" cried Pig.

Goose landed beside her.
"Pig," said Goose, "that was a very good try."
"Yes," huffed Pig, "that was my best try."

Goose and Pig stood in the road
and were silent for a bit.
The sun was hot. Pig was very thirsty.
"Goose?" said Pig.
"Yes?" answered Goose.
"I have never seen a pig fly," admitted Pig.
"I have never seen a pig fly," agreed Goose.

“I would look very dumb,” stated Pig.

“You might look a little silly,” suggested Goose.

Pig put her head back and laughed loudly.
Goose held his belly and laughed, too.
They rolled in the road
and snorted and honked.
They laughed until they cried.

"Goose?" said Pig finally.

"Pig?" answered Goose.

"Let's go eat my picnic by the pond."

"That," said Goose, "is a very good idea!"

"Yes," agreed Pig, "I thought so, too."

A Picnic Lunch

Pig and Goose found a cool spot by the pond.
It was under a big oak tree.
The shade was deep green.
The pond was dark blue.
High above, the sun glowed hot orange.
Pig unpacked the picnic.
"Lunch is served," announced Pig.
Pig took a big bite of pickle.
Pig looked thoughtful.

"Goose," said Pig, "spring is the best season."

"Yes," said Goose.

Pig took another bite.

"And so is summer," she said.

"I agree," said Goose.

"Just as nice as fall," said Pig, as she chewed.

"Always," said Goose.

"And perfect like winter," declared Pig
with a swallow.
"Exactly," said Goose.
"Aren't we lucky," asked Pig,
"to have the best season every season?"
"Yes," said Goose.
Pig sighed. "I think so, too."

After lunch, Pig and Goose grew quiet.
They watched the sun play on the water.
They watched the wind play in the new leaves.
Everything whispered and waved and danced.
Pig grew sleepy.
"Nap time," said Pig.
Before long, Pig was fast asleep
under the big oak tree.

Pig dreamed she was flying with Goose.
They flew over hills and fields.
They flew over barns and rivers.
They flew over a pond with a big oak tree.

When Pig awoke, she yawned
and stretched and smiled.

She looked around for Goose.
Goose was gone!
"Goose?" said Pig.
"GOOSE!?" yelled Pig.

Then, far out in the pond,
Pig saw a small white dot.

The dot got bigger

and bigger.

The dot hopped out of the water right by Pig!
The dot was not a dot at all.

It was Goose!

"Wow!" exclaimed Pig. "You can swim, too!"
Goose blushed. "Gosh," he said,
"it is nothing. All geese can swim."

"Well, I can't," said Pig with a sigh.
"Swimming is so elegant.
So graceful. So quiet.
I am none of those things." Pig frowned.

"But," said Goose, "you are other things."

Pig's face brightened.

"You are right," she said.

Pig looked up at the young green leaves.

"Goose," said Pig. "I am having a party.

It is my First-Day-of-Spring Party.

It is tonight. Would you like to come?"

"Oh!" cried Goose. "I would love to come!"

"Goody gumdrops!" said Pig.

Pig told Goose where her house was.

She told Goose when to come.

Then Pig hurried home to cook for the party.

The Party

It was cool outside, and the sky was purple dark when Goose arrived at Pig's home. Warm light was shining from Pig's windows. Goose could already hear happy talking and laughing coming from inside.

Goose knocked.

The door swung open.

"Goose!" exclaimed Pig. "Welcome to my First-Day-of-Spring Party!"

"Thank you," said Goose.

"Everyone," said Pig, "this is Goose!"
Pig introduced Goose to Cat and Rabbit,
Hen and Turtle, and Frog.
That night Goose spent three whole hours
at Pig's house.
It felt like three minutes.

Pig cooked many delicious things.
She roasted squash and new potatoes.
She fixed snap peas and green lettuce.
She made sweet tea with mint.

For dessert, Pig made her famous
oatmeal cake with ginger.
It was all so tasty.
Every last crumb was eaten.

While they ate, Pig told great stories.
She told old stories and new stories,
sad stories and happy stories.

When she talked, everybody listened.
When she told jokes, everybody laughed.
But always, no matter what,
Pig laughed the most.
Pig was so much fun.

After dinner, Pig put on spicy music,
and the dancing began.
Rabbit danced with Turtle.
Cat danced with Hen.
Goose danced with Frog.
Pig danced with *everyone*.

After the dancing, Pig said,
"One more thing. Come with me."
Everyone got up.
Everyone went outside.
Everyone looked to the sky.
The stars were bright and white and crisp.
There were thousands. There were *millions*.
"It is the first day of spring," said Pig,
"and the stars have come to our party."

When the party was over,
everyone thanked Pig and said good night.
Goose stayed to help Pig clean up.
There was a lot to clean up.
It took a long time.

While they worked, Goose grew silent.

Finally, as he dried the last dish, Goose spoke.

"Pig," whispered Goose, "you are *wonderful*."

"Really?" Pig said, blushing. "*Me*?"

"Yes," said Goose, "you."

"I am very happy to have you as my
new friend," said Goose.

"I am very happy to have you as my
new friend," said Pig.

Goose smiled. Pig laughed.

"I should go home," said Goose. "It is late."

"Yes," said Pig. "It is late. Good night, Goose."

"Good night, Pig," said Goose.

Goose walked out
into the purple dark.
Pig closed the door.

Pig opened the door.
"Wait!" she cried.
"Yes?" said Goose.

"Shall we have a picnic tomorrow?" Pig asked.
"By the pond? Under the big oak tree?"
"Oh, yes!" said Goose. "I love picnics!"
"Goody," said Pig with a laugh.
"Goody gumdrops!"